2014

BASKETBALL

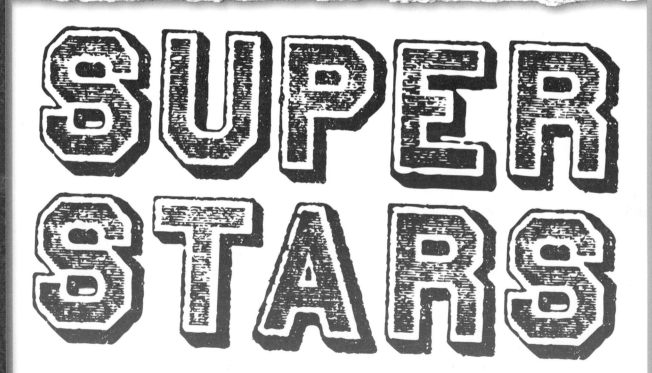

SUPER STARS

By K.C. Kelley

SCHOLASTIC

© 2013

ISBN 978-0-545-64376-4

Photo Editor: Cynthia Carris

12 11 10 9 8 7 6 5 4 3 2 1   14 15 16 17 18 19/ 0

Printed in the U.S.A.   40
First printing, January 2014

TABLE OF CONTENTS

CARMELO ANTHONY

FORWARD   NEW YORK KNICKS

HEIGHT: 6-8   **WEIGHT: 230 LBS**   **ALL-STAR GAMES: 6**

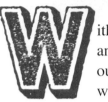With an ability to score in any situation—inside, outside, long-range, dunks, whatever—Carmelo "Melo" Anthony is one of the NBA's most versatile scoring machines. After a solid career with the Denver Nuggets, Anthony joined the New York Knicks in 2011 and has blossomed in the Big Apple. He used all of his moves and more to win the 2013 NBA scoring title, averaging 28.7 points per game, just shy of his career best.

To reach those NBA heights, though, he had to work hard on and off the court.

Anthony went to Syracuse University, and as an 18-year-old freshman, he helped them win the 2003 NCAA championship. In the Final Four, Anthony averaged 26.5 points per game and was named the Most Outstanding Player.

After only one year in college, Anthony made the move to the pros. The Nuggets made him the third overall pick in the 2003 NBA Draft and handed him the role of high-scoring star. He didn't disappoint. Melo has never averaged fewer than 20.8 points in a season ever since.

He was traded to the Knicks in 2011 and has done even better! In 2012–13, the Knicks were one of the NBA's highest-scoring teams, so look for more Melo in the seasons ahead.

> "Playing in New York has been a lot of fun. It has ups and downs, smiles and frowns, but at the end of the day it's been a lovely experience. It's been a lot of fun."

THREE POINTS:

- Set Big East freshman scoring record at Syracuse (22.2 ppg)
- Won gold medal with U.S. Olympic team in 2008 and 2012
- In a 2008 game, tied an NBA record with 33 points in one quarter

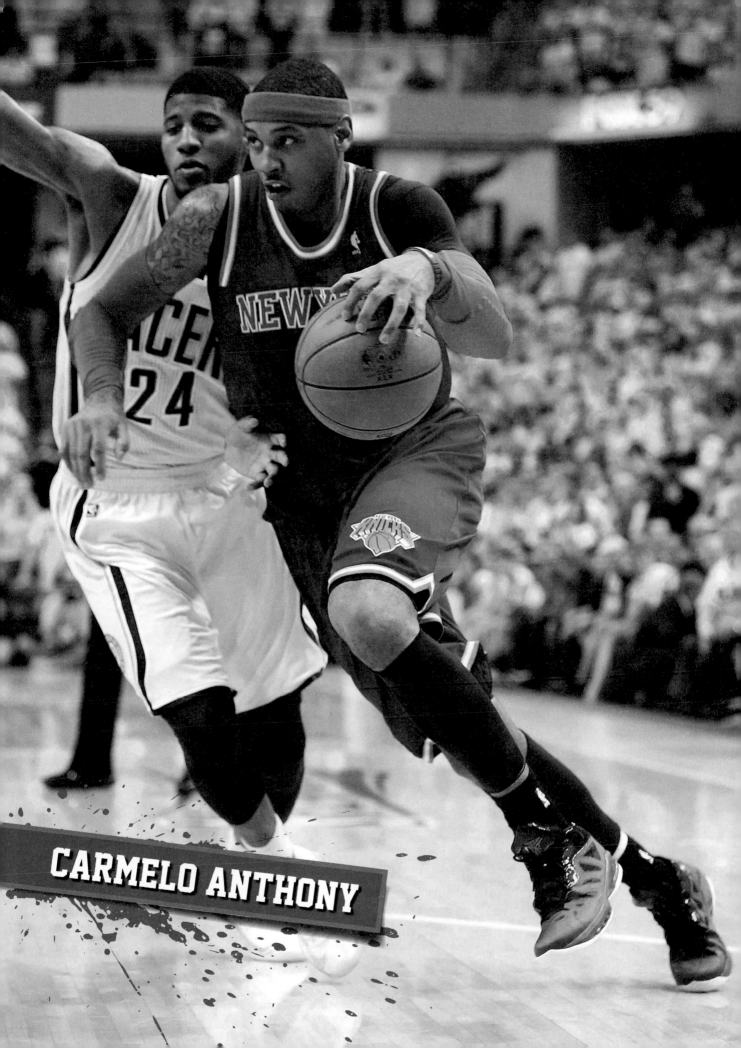

CARMELO ANTHONY

KOBE BRYANT

GUARD | LOS ANGELES LAKERS

| HEIGHT: 6-6 | WEIGHT: 205 LBS | ALL-STAR GAMES: 15 |

 In any discussion of the "best players in the NBA," you have to include Kobe Bryant. He's grown from a high-school sensation to become one of the all-time best. In 1996, he jumped right from a Pennsylvania prep school to the NBA. Bryant was following in the NBA footsteps of his dad, Joe "Jellybean" Bryant, who played for several NBA teams and in Europe.

Bryant joined the Lakers the same season as all-time great Shaquille O'Neal. When coach Phil Jackson came along in 1999, they became a super team. L.A. won three straight NBA championships from 2000 to 2002. Bryant was the slashing point guard, scoring and dishing with insane moves. O'Neal was the towering inside force.

"[If everyone comes back healthy we can] win a championship, no doubt about it."

But Shaq left before the 2005–06 season and it was up to Kobe to become the Lakers' main weapon. Bryant won back-to-back scoring championships in 2006 and 2007. Joined by power forward Pau Gasol, Bryant led the Lakers back to the top of the NBA in 2009 and 2010. That gave him five NBA rings, one fewer than Michael Jordan . . . but one more than Shaq!

How much do the Lakers depend on Bryant now? Since 2005–06, he has led the NBA in field-goal attempts every year but one. He missed the 2013 playoffs with an ankle injury and the Lakers were swept for the first time since 1967. But Bryant has come back before, and he should be back on the court, scoring and starring for the Lakers, later in the season.

THREE POINTS:

- Middle name is Bean, after dad's nickname
- Has been NBA All-Star Game MVP four times
- Has led NBA in total points four times

KOBE BRYANT

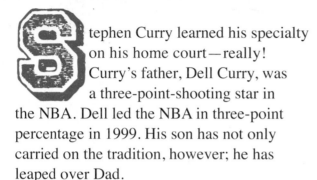

STEPHEN CURRY

GUARD | GOLDEN STATE WARRIORS

| HEIGHT: 6-3 | WEIGHT: 185 LBS | ALL-STAR GAMES: 0 |

Stephen Curry learned his specialty on his home court—really! Curry's father, Dell Curry, was a three-point-shooting star in the NBA. Dell led the NBA in three-point percentage in 1999. His son has not only carried on the tradition, however; he has leaped over Dad.

Stephen Curry was a high-school star in North Carolina, but he was only six feet tall then. Big college programs didn't think he could make it at his size, so he went to nearby Davidson College. He showed that size didn't matter! As a sophomore, he set an NCAA record with 162 three-point field goals. As a junior, Curry grew to 6-3 and led the NCAA in scoring with 28.6 points per game.

The Warriors made him the seventh pick in the 2009 draft, and he was a starter from his first game. He was one of the top rookies in the league. In his second season, Curry led the NBA in free-throw percentage and was in the top 10 in three-pointers made in 2010 and 2011.

Curry's rapid rise was briefly stopped in 2012 by an ankle injury. He missed the final 40 games of the 2011–12 season.

Curry must have enjoyed the rest. When he returned for the 2012–13 season, he started shooting threes . . . and never stopped. By the time the season was over, Curry had set a new single-season record with 272 three-point buckets. He also led the league with 600 three-point attempts.

The hot-shooting guard also guided the Warriors to their best record since 2008. They made it to the conference semifinals before losing to the Spurs. With his proud dad looking on, Curry will continue to pour in the points from "way downtown."

> ## "My dad knew I had [my success] in me, but for him, it's been great to see me put it all together like he did for 16 years [in the NBA]. I could see how proud he was."

THREE POINTS:

- Real first name is *Wardell*; *Stephen* is middle name
- Led NCAA in scoring in 2008-09 with 28.6 ppg
- Member of 2010 NBA All-Rookie Team

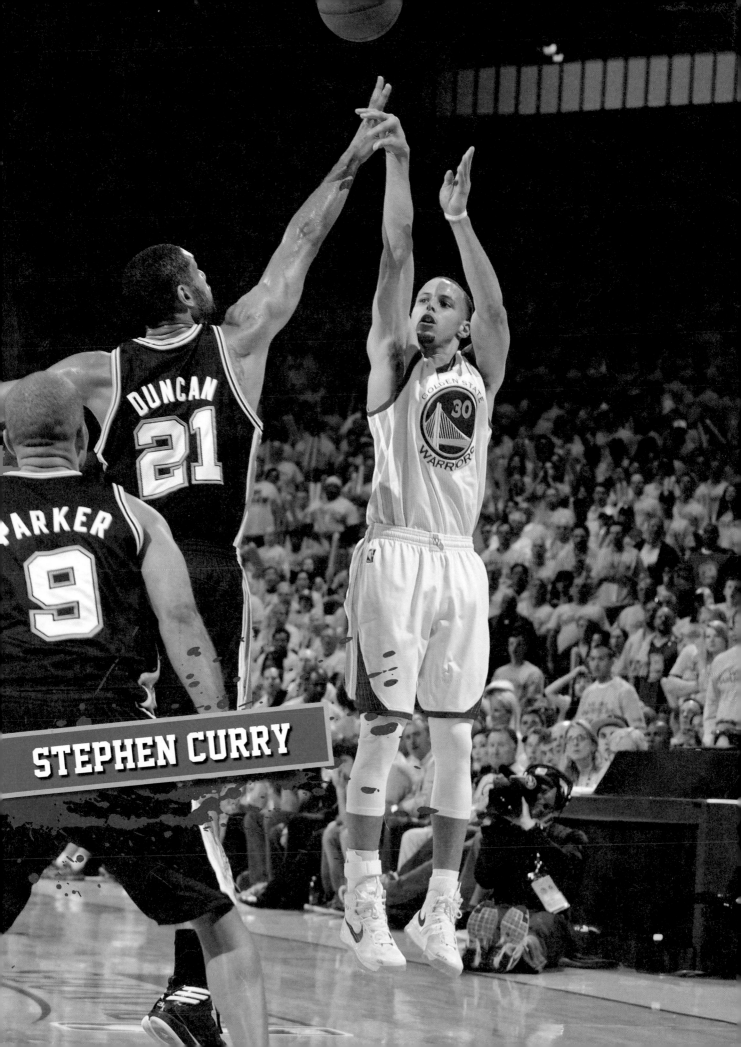

STEPHEN CURRY

TIM DUNCAN

FORWARD/CENTER | SAN ANTONIO SPURS

HEIGHT: 6-11	WEIGHT: 255 LBS	ALL-STAR GAMES: 14

Duncan has an unusual background for an NBA star. He grew up as a champion swimmer in the U.S. Virgin Islands. But he took up hoops in high school, and now NBA opponents probably wish he had stayed in the pool! After being named college player of the year at Wake Forest, Duncan joined the Spurs in 1997 and has since become one of the top power forwards of all time.

After being chosen first overall by San Antonio, Duncan helped the team improve by 32 games, the biggest one-season leap ever. He was named the 1998 Rookie of the Year. Together, the Spurs and Duncan began one of the biggest dynasties in the NBA. The Spurs won their first NBA title in 1999 and then won three more in the next eight seasons. Duncan earned a pair of NBA MVP awards (2002 and 2003) and has been named first-team All-NBA 10 times. In addition, the Spurs have made

the playoffs each year Duncan has been in the league. Their most recent success was an NBA Finals berth in 2013, though they fell to LeBron James and the Heat.

Duncan's greatest skills are in the paint, where he has a wide variety of scoring moves. Five times he has been in the top 10 in scoring. On the glass, he's unstoppable. He led the NBA in rebounding in 2002, and has been among the top five rebounders eight other times.

Wait, there's more! Duncan is also one of the top defenders in the league, taking on the best centers and opposing power forwards and shutting them down. Duncan has been on the NBA's All-Defensive First Team eight times and is the NBA's active leader in career blocks!

Though he's not a fiery, outspoken person, his quiet, behind-the-scenes leadership has been a key part of the Spurs' longtime success.

THREE POINTS:

- 2000 NBA All-Star Game MVP
- 1999, 2003, and 2005 NBA Finals MVP
- 2002 and 2003 NBA MVP

"We're right in the mix. We're pushing hard. Nobody expected us to be where we are. We're staying in the mix and we're excited about it."

TIM DUNCAN

KEVIN DURANT

FORWARD   OKLAHOMA CITY THUNDER

HEIGHT: 6-9   **WEIGHT: 235 LBS**   **ALL-STAR GAMES: 4**

When you watch Kevin Durant play, you often have this thought: *How can someone so big and so tall shoot so sweetly?* The two-time scoring champion combines fly-to-the-rack size with a deadly outside shooting touch. He has used those skills to turn the Thunder into one of the NBA's best teams.

Durant grew up near Washington, D.C., and was a solid basketball player even before high school. He constantly practiced his ballhandling and basketball moves. After one year in high school, though, he grew five inches! As a taller player, he kept the skills he had developed when he was shorter.

He went to the University of Texas after an awesome high-school career. Though only a freshman, he won several awards as the college player of the year! The NBA was the next big step; he was the second overall pick of the 2007 NBA Draft after just one college season. The Seattle SuperSonics chose him and he rewarded them by being named the 2008 NBA Rookie of the Year. The team moved to Oklahoma City after Durant's first season. They changed their name to the Thunder and Durant became the focus of their offense.

By his third season, his great skill with the ball and his outside shooting had made him the NBA's top scorer. He led the NBA in points-per-game in 2010, 2011, and 2012. The Thunder followed their big man's success, making the playoffs every year starting in 2009. They got as far as the NBA Finals in 2012 before losing to the Heat.

Durant continues to score in bunches, but he is also growing as a team leader. The hot-shooting 19-year-old has matured into one of the top all-around players in the league.

"I'm always going to fight for the game I love. I'm going to claw until the last buzzer sounds."

THREE POINTS:

- 2006 All-American in high school
- 2012 NBA All-Star Game MVP
- Led NBA in free-throw percentage in 2012-13

KEVIN DURANT

PAUL GEORGE

FORWARD | INDIANA PACERS

HEIGHT: 6-8	WEIGHT: 221 LBS	ALL-STAR GAMES:1

 From the time players are just starting out, coaches tell them to try to get better every game, every season. Indiana Pacers forward Paul George took that advice to heart . . . and slammed it home! The NBA's Most Improved Player in 2013 has changed from a solid, dependable forward to one of the best young players in the league. George has increased his points per game, his rebounds, and his assists in each of his three full seasons.

It has been a steady climb to the top. In high school in Palmdale, California, he was not a star until his final season—but then he averaged 25 points per game! In college at Fresno State, he didn't really blossom until his junior year. And though he was drafted

"Well, hopefully this is just the beginning. There is a lot more in store . . ."

tenth overall by the Pacers in 2010, he did not become a full-time starter until the 2012–13 season.

For the Pacers, whom George led to the 2013 Eastern Conference Finals, it was worth the wait. Not only can he score from anywhere, he's among the toughest defenders in the NBA. That's a powerful one-two punch.

Though he's young, George knows what he has to do. "Moving forward, I [want] that pressure, I want to be that go-to guy," he told ESPN.com. "When something's not going well offensively, I want to be able to say, 'I want the ball.'"

Give him the ball? The way George is improving, that's something the Pacers will be happy to do!

THREE POINTS:

- Was inspired to play in college by older sister Teiosha, who played at Pepperdine

- Scored 17 points in first All-Star Game in 2013

- Named third-team ALL-NBA in 2013

PAUL GEORGE

BLAKE GRIFFIN

FORWARD | LOS ANGELES CLIPPERS

| HEIGHT: 6-10 | WEIGHT: 251 LBS | ALL-STAR GAMES: 3 |

**H**ere is most of what you need to know about Blake Griffin: He once leaped over a car to make a dunk.

Okay, it was just a slam-dunk contest, but still . . . he jumped over a car!

That sort of high-flying, rim-rattling power has made Griffin one of the most exciting players in the NBA. Fans and teammates alike marvel at his ongoing series of dunks, slams, and ripped rebounds.

Griffin played high-school basketball in his native Oklahoma for a team his dad coached. Together they won four straight state championships. Griffin then gained national attention for his dunks at the University of Oklahoma. As a sophomore, he was named to the All-American team and won all the major national player of the year awards.

It was no surprise that the Clippers took him with the first overall pick in 2009. But then his rocket ride to the top stalled. He injured his knee while playing summer ball and had to have surgery. The injury made him miss the 2009–10 NBA season. Could the big man come back?

Griffin worked hard to get better and the hard work paid off. In 2010–11, he was the first rookie to start the All-Star game since 1998. He won the Slam Dunk Contest with that car-leaping bucket. It was no surprise when he was named the 2011 NBA Rookie of the Year.

Since then, Griffin has teamed with guard Chris Paul to make the Clippers one of the league's up-and-coming teams. L.A. had its best season ever in 2013, and George can't wait to rise above the rim again to bring more wins to Clippers fans.

" . . . I know I have to be patient—I know it's a process to get better every year and enjoy the ride."

THREE POINTS:

- All-American power forward in high school
- Scored a Clippers team-record 47 points in 2010 game
- Led Clippers to most wins ever in 2013

BLAKE GRIFFIN

JAMES HARDEN

FORWARD | HOUSTON ROCKETS

| HEIGHT: 6-5 | WEIGHT: 220 LBS | ALL-STAR GAMES: 1 |

It's the beard, right? That's the first thing you notice about James Harden—that awesome fuzzy beard. The beard is so famous that fans in Oklahoma City, his first NBA stop, used to wear fake beards to games in his honor.

But NBA opponents know that there is much more to this lefty sharpshooter than wild facial hair. In his fourth season—and his first as the "go-to guy" on the Houston Rockets—Harden had his best season as a pro.

Harden grew up near Los Angeles and had to overcome childhood asthma. By his junior year in high school, Harden was one of the best players in the state. He led his team to back-to-back California championships and earned a scholarship to Arizona State. Chosen third overall by Oaklahoma City, Harden became a key man as the Thunder reached 50

"I try to always get better by watching and learning and putting what I see into my style of play."

wins for the first time. He was so good at his job, which was coming off the bench to provide scoring punch, that he was named NBA Sixth Man of the Year in 2012. More importantly, the Thunder made it to the NBA Finals, where they lost to the Heat. Harden's contributions, especially in scoring, were key to the team's rise.

However, after the season, the Thunder traded him to the Rockets. In Houston, Harden was not the sixth man . . . he was THE man. He led the Rockets in scoring and was second in assists behind guard Jeremy Lin. Houston made the playoffs for the first time since 2008.

Scoring punch, team leadership, all-around talent—there's lots more to Harden than his famous beard.

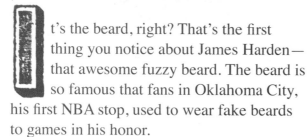

THREE POINTS:

- Named a high school All-American as a senior
- Has led his team to NBA playoffs every year of his career
- In 2013, tied a career single-game high with 46 points

JAMES HARDEN

LEBRON JAMES

FORWARD   MIAMI HEAT

HEIGHT: 6-8   **WEIGHT: 250 LBS**   **ALL-STAR GAMES: 9**

he NBA is full of dominating players, athletes who can take over a game by themselves. But the one player who does that best is the reigning NBA MVP and two-time champ: LeBron "King" James. Nearly all experts call him the best player in the NBA now. But is he the best ever?

James led his high-school team to two state championships and was the national player of the year as a senior. He was already nationally known when he chose to skip college and join the NBA at 18.

In 2003, LeBron was drafted by his hometown team, the Cleveland Cavaliers. James was Rookie of the Year and played on his first Olympic team when he was just 19. In his second season, he was third in the league in scoring. The next year, he was the youngest player ever to average 30 points in a season. By 2006, he had led the Cavs to their first NBA Finals, though they lost to the Spurs. All along, he was showing the high-scoring skills and powerful defense that would be part of his all-around game.

After helping the United States win gold in the 2008 Olympics, James was the 2009 NBA MVP. But he felt that he could not become a champion in Cleveland. Before the 2010–11 season, James was free to sign with any team. They all wanted him, but in a national broadcast on ESPN, he announced "The Decision": James joined the Miami Heat.

"We've been able to persevere and win back-to-back championships."

Along with Chris Bosh and Dwyane Wade, also drafted in 2003, James led the Heat to the NBA Finals, but they lost to Dallas. They used that as fuel to improve and "The Big Three" turned the Heat into champs, winning back-to-back titles in 2012 and 2013. James won two more NBA MVP awards and dominated in the playoffs, winning games with amazing scoring and impressive defense.

Is he the best player of all time? Check back in a couple more championship seasons to find the answer.

THREE POINTS:

- Led NBA in scoring in 2008; has finished second in total points eight times
- 2006 and 2008 NBA All-Star Game MVP
- 2012 and 2013 NBA Finals MVP

LEBRON JAMES

TONY PARKER
GUARD | SAN ANTONIO SPURS

HEIGHT: 6-2	WEIGHT: 185 LBS	ALL-STAR GAMES: 5

Tony Parker's childhood was much different than most NBA players'. Parker was born in Bruges, Belgium, and grew up in France. Tony's dad was a pro basketball player from Chicago. Each summer the family would return there for visits, and young Tony would watch Michael Jordan do his stuff for the Bulls. Inspired by Jordan and taught by his dad, Tony became a star in French pro leagues when he was just a teenager.

In 2001, he was chosen by the Spurs with the final pick of the NBA Draft's first round. He was not expected to start, but his talent showed through quickly. He drove the Spurs' offense and was named to the NBA All-Rookie team. In his second season, the Spurs won the NBA championship. San Antonio would win two more titles in the next four seasons, and Parker's all-around play was a big part of the team's success.

He has great outside shooting ability, but he is also fearless going to the hoop. Combine those skills with the big-man inside game of star Tim Duncan and the Spurs have a powerful one-two punch.

In 2013, Parker reached the NBA Finals again. Although Parker made a huge shot to win Game 1, the team lost in seven games to the Heat. After the season ended, Parker played in the Eurobasket tournament, leading the French national team to their first-ever victory. Between the playoffs and the tourney, that's a whole lot of games played in a year! He'll be 32 during the 2014–15 season, but Parker's chances of returning to the Finals are *trés bien*!

THREE POINTS:

- Led French junior national team to European title and was MVP

- Was named 2007 NBA Finals MVP

- Has never played on an NBA team with a losing record

> "We all keep our ego for ourselves, and make the **team most important.**"

TONY PARKER

CHRIS PAUL

GUARD　LOS ANGELES CLIPPERS

HEIGHT: 6-0	WEIGHT: 175 LBS	ALL-STAR GAMES: 6

A superstar at every level, Chris Paul has found great success in all aspects of his game. Growing up in North Carolina, Paul was outstanding in high school, earning All-American honors and being named Mr. Basketball in his home state. He moved to Wake Forest in North Carolina for the 2003–04 season. He wound up a first-team All-American as a sophomore before moving to the NBA.

Paul joined the New Orleans Hornets after they made him the fourth overall selection in 2005. The point guard quickly became the key to the team's offense, and he was the 2006 NBA Rookie of the Year. In 2008, he led the team to its best record ever and first playoff spot in five seasons.

After the 2011 season, however, a huge trade sent Paul's career in a whole new direction—west. He was traded with several other players to the Los Angeles Clippers, a team that had struggled for many years. Three thousand miles from home, Paul blossomed in L.A. For one thing, he had a huge target for his passes in slam-dunking forward Blake Griffin. For another, he had a new crosstown rivalry with Lakers star Kobe Bryant to spur him on. Paul and Griffin teamed up to make the Clippers the hottest young team in the league. In their first season together, they carried the Clippers to the playoffs for the first time in six years and then to a playoff win over Memphis. In 2013, Paul guided the Clippers to the best record in team history! Clippers fans were jazzed (and not the Utah kind) when Paul signed to play in L.A. for five more years.

> **"The hardest part about my son getting older and knowing the game is that he can let me know what I did wrong. After we lose, he'll see me and say, 'Daddy, you lost.'"**

THREE POINTS:

- Led NBA in assists in 2008 and 2009
- Led NBA in steals five times
- Was MVP of 2013 NBA All-Star Game

CHRIS PAUL

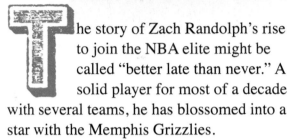

ZACH RANDOLPH

FORWARD | MEMPHIS GRIZZLIES

HEIGHT: 6-9	WEIGHT: 260 LBS	ALL-STAR GAMES: 2

The story of Zach Randolph's rise to join the NBA elite might be called "better late than never." A solid player for most of a decade with several teams, he has blossomed into a star with the Memphis Grizzlies.

Randolph grew up in Indiana, a state that is crazy for basketball. He was recruited by many schools, but chose to head north to Michigan State. In 2001, Randolph's powerful inside game helped the Spartans reach the Final Four.

He was chosen in the first round of the 2002 NBA Draft by Portland. By his third season, he was a starter and averaged more than 20 points—the first of five times he would do that in his career (so far!). In 2004, he was named the NBA's Most Improved Player, but he knew that he could get even better. In 2007, he was traded to the Knicks, who sent him to the Clippers in 2008. The Clippers moved him to Memphis, and that's where Randolph has established himself.

With the Grizzlies, he has used his powerful rebounding skills to give the team a strong inside game, joined by super-defender Marc Gasol. In 2010, the veteran Randolph made his first All-Star Game, becoming only the second Memphis player ever in the contest. In 2011, Randolph helped Memphis reach the playoffs for the first time in five seasons. Finally, in 2012–13, the Grizzlies set a team record with 56 wins and made the conference finals. Though he does not score as much as he used to, Randolph contributes in other ways—whatever it takes to win!

THREE POINTS:

- Was named All-American in high school
- 2011 ALL-NBA third team—first in Grizzlies history
- Led NBA in offensive rebounds twice

> "I've been the underdog my whole life. It's good to be the underdog sometimes."

ZACH RANDOLPH

DERRICK ROSE

GUARD | CHICAGO BULLS

| HEIGHT: 6-3 | WEIGHT: 190 LBS | ALL-STAR GAMES: 3 |

When you're the first overall pick in the NBA Draft, and you take over as the "face" of the Chicago Bulls, you have some big sneakers to fill. Fortunately for Bulls fans, All-Star guard Derrick Rose has been up to the task. Since they made him that top pick in 2008, Rose has become one of the league's top talents at the all-important point guard spot.

He was an easy choice for the Bulls—a hometown player with huge pro potential. And he showed that, in this case, the easy choice was the right one. Rose was the 2009 Rookie of the Year after averaging 16.8 points per game, but he was just getting started. The next year, he made his first All-Star game, the first player from the Bulls to do so in 11 seasons.

In 2010–11, he and the Bulls really clicked. Rose led the team with 25 points per game, while also dishing out 7.7 assists per game. He smoothly guided the team to the best record in the Eastern Conference, and its most wins since Michael Jordan left the team. Though he was disappointed their playoff run ended, he was happy to be named the 2011 NBA MVP. He beat out stars such as LeBron James and Kobe Bryant for the honor.

Unfortunately, a knee injury the following season (2012–13) kept Rose off the court until the 2013–14 season. He's determined, however. "There's only one goal this year," he said, "to win an NBA championship."

"I'm just going to react and play the game. Every day I wake up and try to be the best player on the court."

THREE POINTS:

- High-school team beat powerful Oak Hill in nationally televised 2007 game
- Named South Region most outstanding player in 2009 NCAA tournament
- Scored career-high 42 points in a pair of 2011 games

DERRICK ROSE

RUSSELL WESTBROOK

GUARD   OKLAHOMA CITY THUNDER

HEIGHT: 6-3   WEIGHT: 187 LBS   ALL-STAR GAMES: 3

You've heard the expression "playing with a chip on his shoulder"? It means a player is out to prove something. In the 2013–14 season, Russell Westbrook will be playing with a chip on his knee. Westbrook hurt his right knee early in the 2013 playoffs. His absence made it hard on his team, and the Thunder lost in the second round to Memphis. Westbrook wanted to be out there, but his injury prevented that. Heading into the new season, he'll be even more fired up than before.

And a fired-up Russell Westbrook is bad news for any opponent.

The super-skilled guard joined the Thunder in 2008 out of UCLA, where he was an All-Pac-10 player and hclped the Bruins reach the Final Four twice. He was actually chosen fourth overall by Oklahoma City just a few days later.

"While I was out [during the playoffs], I wished I was playing, but I tried to learn while I was watching."

From the start, Westbrook was a big part of the Thunder. His steady and creative play as the team's point guard energized the team. By his second season, led by Westbrook and high-scoring partner Kevin Durant, the Thunder had become one of the league's best teams. Westbrook's ability to cut to the basket opened up passing lanes to Durant. If opponents stuck with the big man, Westbrook drove to the hoop himself. Along with his scoring power, Westbrook was very dependable. In his five NBA seasons, he has not missed a single regular-season game.

He had his best season in 2012–13 before the injury happened. He was sixth in the NBA in scoring and seventh in assists. Westbrook should be back as good as ever, and he'll watch the chips fall where they will!

THREE POINTS:

- Grew seven inches in high school; averaged 25.1 ppg as senior
- Won 2012 Olympic gold medal with U.S. team
- Twice named to All-NBA second team

RUSSELL WESTBROOK

TEAMS OF THE NBA

EASTERN CONFERENCE

Atlantic Division

Boston Celtics

Brooklyn Nets

New York Knicks

Philadelphia 76ers

Toronto Raptors

Central Division

Chicago Bulls

Cleveland Cavaliers

Detroit Pistons

Indiana Pacers

Milwaukee Bucks

Southeast Division

Atlanta Hawks

Charlotte Bobcats

Miami Heat

Orlando Magic

Washington Wizards

WESTERN CONFERENCE

Northwest Division

Denver Nuggets

Minnesota Timberwolves

Oklahoma City Thunder

Portland Trail Blazers

Utah Jazz

Pacific Division

Golden State Warriors

Los Angeles Clippers

Los Angeles Lakers

Phoenix Suns

Sacramento Kings

Southwest Division

Dallas Mavericks

Houston Rockets

Memphis Grizzlies

New Orleans Pelicans

San Antonio Spurs